This book belongs to:
Jack Cowie
+Mia Strac...

6
2 St marden
road
...
3

SIMON AND SCHUSTER
First published in Great Britain in 2011 by Simon & Schuster UK Ltd
1st Floor, 222 Gray's Inn Road, London WC1X 8HB
A CBS Company

All titles included were originally published in the USA as individual
titles by Simon Spotlight, an imprint of Simon & Schuster
Children's Division, New York.

A CIP catalogue record for this book is
available from the British Library

ISBN   978-0-85707-126-2

Printed in China

10 9 8 7 6 5 4 3 2 1

www.simonandschuster.co.uk
and www.nick.co.uk

Surf's Up, SPONGEBOB!

SIMON AND SCHUSTER

Contents:

SpongeBob SquarePants

Class Confusion

by Sarah Willson
illustrated by Robert Dress

"SpongeBob, look out!" shrieked Mrs Puff. But it was too late.
SCREEEECH! CRASH! BOOM! BOOM! BOOM!

"Oops. Sorry, Mrs Puff," said SpongeBob. "I guess I forgot to put my blinker on. Looks like I failed my boating test . . . again."

"I'm calling in sick tomorrow," Mrs Puff muttered. "I need a little 'me' time."

9

The next day SpongeBob arrived early for boating school, as usual. He breathed in deeply as he entered the front doors. "Behold the halls of learning," he said to himself.

"And here is the fountain of learning, which I drink from every day!" He took a sip from the drinking fountain, then continued down the hall.

At the classroom door SpongeBob's voice quavered. "And inside that room is the one who makes it all happen."

Slowly he pushed open the door. "Yes, indeed, inside this room is my teacher, the one and only Mrs. . . . AHHHHHHHH!"

Mrs Puff was not at her desk! Instead there was . . . a *substitute!*
"Wh-wh-where's Mrs Puff?" SpongeBob finally asked.
The substitute did not even look up from the magazine he was reading.
"Out today," he said, turning a page. "Have a seat."

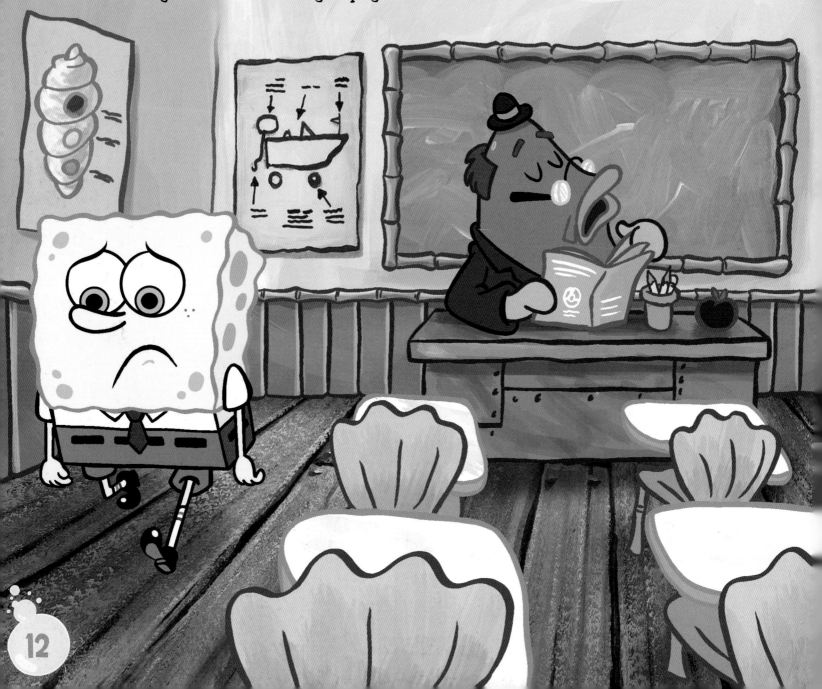

SpongeBob sank heavily into his chair.

"Pssssst!" said a voice next to him. It was Horace.

"I have a really funny idea," whispered Horace. "Let's play a trick on the sub! I'll pretend to be you, and you pretend to be me! Okay? It'll be hilarious!" Horace said, sniggering.

"Uh, I guess so," said SpongeBob. He really didn't mind.

The substitute stood up. He was holding a clipboard. "Time to take attendance," he said. "Susie?"

"Here!" said Susie.

"Franco?"

"Here!" said Franco.

"SpongeBob?"

"HERE!" yelled Horace, before SpongeBob could say anything.

"Horace?" There was a pause. "Is Horace here today?"

SpongeBob felt a poke in his ribs. "Oh, yeah. Here," said SpongeBob, as Horace sniggered some more.

The substitute began passing out pieces of paper. "Today you're supposed to take a test," he said.

Everyone groaned, except SpongeBob, whose eyes shone with excitement. A test!

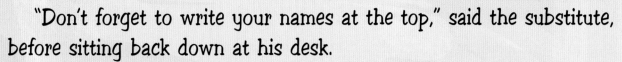

"Don't forget to write your names at the top," said the substitute, before sitting back down at his desk.

"Pssst!" whispered Horace to SpongeBob. Horace pointed to his own test where he had written the name *SpongeBob*. Then Horace pointed at SpongeBob's paper.

SpongeBob wrote *Horace* at the top of his own test.

After the test, the substitute told the class, "Okay, now, open your manuals and read or something."

SpongeBob's hand shot up. "Mrs Puff usually reviews the homework with us, and then after that she teaches us the lesson of the day and whoever has the most class participation — usually me — gets to stay after school and clap the erasers."

The substitute blinked at SpongeBob. "Is that right" — he looked down at his clipboard — "Horace? Well, *I* do things a bit differently. But you just reminded me. Your teacher left me a list of students who are to stay after school for extra help." He glanced at a sheet of paper. "Oh. Just one student. That would be you, SpongeBob." He pointed at Horace.

Horace looked over at SpongeBob and winked.

After school SpongeBob walked home very slowly.
"Hey, SpongeBob!" called Patrick. "Why the sad face?"

"Mrs Puff wasn't at school today," SpongeBob began, "and there was a sub who didn't do anything the right way, and I was supposed to stay after school for extra help, but Horace was pretending to be me so he got to stay and I–," SpongeBob burst into tears.

Patrick patted his friend on the back. "Don't worry, SpongeBob," he said. "I'm sure Mrs Puff will be back tomorrow and everything will be back to normal. You'll be failing another driving test before you know it!"

"I hope so," SpongeBob said, sniffling.

The next day SpongeBob held his breath as he entered the classroom. There, sitting at her desk, was his beloved Mrs Puff! She was looking well-rested.

"Oh, Mrs Puff!" gushed SpongeBob. "I sure am glad to see you!"

Mrs Puff smiled. "Yes, I feel very refreshed after my, um . . . *sick day*," she said.

"Mrs Puff, the sub forgot to give us homework, even though I reminded him three times!" said SpongeBob.

But Mrs Puff wasn't listening. She was staring at a note. "Hmm . . . it seems that the substitute gave you all the *final exam* by mistake. And instead of keeping one student after school for extra help, he sent that student to retake his driving test."

All the colour suddenly drained from her face. "And that student *passed* his driving test!"

"Who was the student?" Franco asked.

Mrs Puff paused before announcing, "It was . . . *SpongeBob!*"

Everyone gasped. SpongeBob had passed his driving test at last!

"I passed! I passed! I passed at last!" SpongeBob yelled to everyone as he walked home — even though he didn't remember taking the test again.

"Hey, no more school, SpongeBob!" said Patrick. "We can play all day!"

SpongeBob grinned. "Yeah, that's great, Patrick! No more homework, no more school, no more . . . Mrs Puff?" Suddenly he realized what this meant.

"Oh, no!" he wailed.

The next day SpongeBob forgot about Mrs Puff for a while. He was too excited to get behind the wheel of a boat all by himself! "I'm ready! I'm ready!" he shouted.

A small crowd had gathered to watch SpongeBob drive alone for the first time. He had rented a limited edition Halibut GXT for this special occasion. Even Mrs Puff was there. "I just don't understand it," said Mrs Puff to herself. "How did he manage to pass his driving test? It's time for me to move far away. I don't want to be around when SpongeBob is driving!"

Vroom-vroom! SpongeBob revved up the engine. Then he noticed his teacher standing nearby. His heart grew heavy. He started to tear up.

"Even though I'm really glad I finally got my license, I sure am going to miss being in your class, Mrs Puff," he said. "Goodbye, Mrs Puff!"

SpongeBob stepped on the gas pedal and the boat flew forward and screeched to a halt in the middle of the intersection.

Suddenly a siren wailed and a police cruiser zoomed up. Two officers hopped out.

"Hey, you didn't stop at that stop sign," said one officer. "Licence, please."

"Yes sir, officer!" SpongeBob replied. "Here it is, brand-new and never used!"

The officer studied the licence. "Hmm . . . seems there's a problem," he said. "You passed the *driving* portion of the boating test, but you failed the written exam."

SpongeBob looked at the test that the officer was holding up. Of course! It was the test that *Horace* had taken, pretending to be SpongeBob, and Horace had failed! And Horace must have passed the driving test . . . *while pretending to be SpongeBob!*

"I'm afraid you'll have to go back to boating school," the officer said.

SpongeBob started to sob. Even Mrs Puff felt bad.

"Aw, don't cry, SpongeBob," said Mrs Puff. "You'll get your licence one day."

"No, Mrs Puff," said SpongeBob. "I'm crying because I'm so happy! I thought I'd never see you again!" And he leapt out of the boat and into the arms of his startled teacher.

"I need a holiday," moaned Mrs Puff softly.

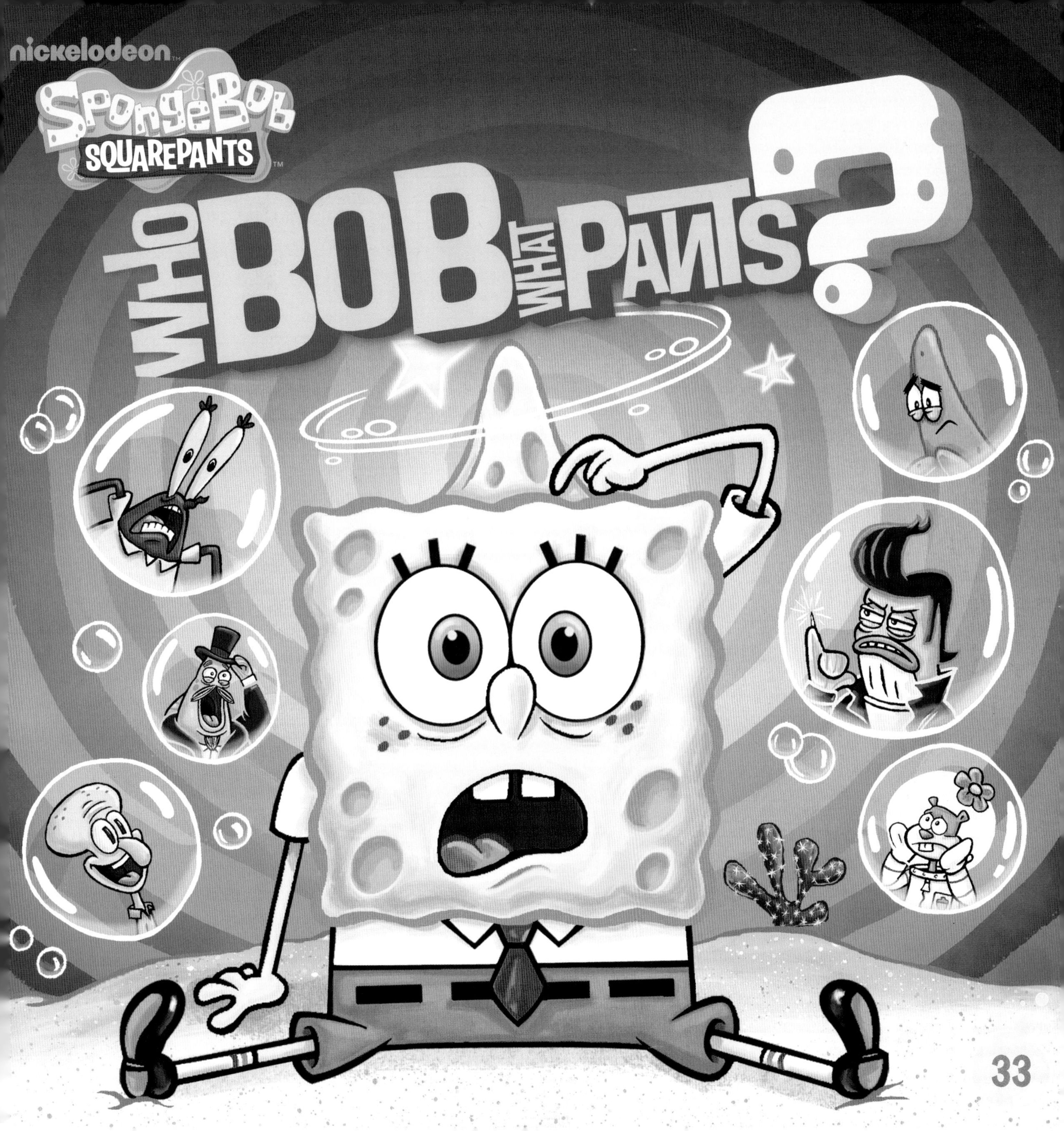
nickelodeon
SpongeBob
SQUAREPANTS
WHO BOB WHAT PANTS?

adapted by Emily Sollinger
based on the screenplay by Casey Alexander,
Zeus Cervas, and Steven Banks
illustrated by Stephen Reed

"Good morning, Gary!" sang SpongeBob. "Isn't life great?" he asked, picking up Gary and hugging him a *little* too tightly. Gary let out a loud growl.

Later, on his way out, SpongeBob bumped right into his best friend, Patrick!

"Oh, hey, Patrick! How goes it?" SpongeBob asked.

"Great, until you showed up," muttered Patrick. "That *was* a cake for my mum's birthday," he continued, pointing to his chocolate-covered belly. "Thanks a lot. Now please just go away!"

SpongeBob frowned and walked away. Next he visited his good friend Squidward. But Squidward just slammed the door in SpongeBob's face! SpongeBob felt even worse than he had before.

SLAM!

He knew Sandy would be happy to see him. But as he walked into her treedome, he tripped and splashed the water from his helmet all over her brand-new robot. Sandy's face turned red with anger.

"Just GO!" she snarled.

There was only one hope left – the Krusty Krab! But as he entered the kitchen, SpongeBob slipped, slid across the floor, and knocked Mr Krabs and his crisp dollar bills right into the fryer!

"If I were you, lad, I'd get as far away from me as possible!" Mr Krabs barked.

Miserable, SpongeBob decided it was time to leave Bikini Bottom forever. "Goodbye, Bikini Bottom," SpongeBob called out. "Goodbye, life as I know it . . ."

After miles of walking, SpongeBob found himself in an unfamiliar place. There were new sounds and scary creatures. It was dark, and suddenly SpongeBob heard a loud noise! Afraid, he ran away as fast as he could. As he ran, SpongeBob tripped on a rock and tumbled down a tall cliff, bumping his head hard on the way down!

Meanwhile, back in Bikini Bottom, Patrick was knocking on SpongeBob's door when Sandy appeared.

"Patrick, where's SpongeBob?" she asked.

"I don't know. I've been knocking on his door for three hours."

Worried, she gave the door a quick karate chop. *Boom!* The door came crashing down. Inside, an oversized Gary let out a "meow."

"Oh, boy!" cried Sandy. "Gary said SpongeBob left a note."

Burp!

GARY

"He's gone! I shouldn't have yelled at SpongeBob," Sandy lamented. "I must have made him feel really bad."

"Me too," said Patrick.

"We have to find him!" said Sandy. "Come on! Let's start searchin'!"

Sandy and Patrick checked the Krusty Krab. SpongeBob wasn't there, but there *were* a lot of hungry customers who wanted their Krabby Patties. Mr Krabs was really worried! He knew that the Krusty Krab couldn't survive without SpongeBob!

"I'm nothing without my number-one fry cook!" said Mr Krabs. "Squidward, I am ordering you to find him. If you don't, you'll be out of a job forever! If you do find him, this jewel-encrusted egg will be yours to keep!"

"A jewel-encrusted egg?" asked Squidward, looking longingly at the egg. "My collection will finally be complete! I am on my way, sir."

Back in the unfamiliar seas, SpongeBob finally opened his eyes and rubbed the large bump on his head. Then he noticed two fish kneeling down, looking at a pile of square pants. He went over to say hello.

"Oh, hello! We were just admiring your clothes!" the fish told him. "These are your brown pants, aren't they?" the fish asked, showing him a pile of brown pants.

"I can't remember. I don't even know my name," said SpongeBob. "All I know is that I hit my head and woke up here."

"That's too bad. Let's call you Cheesehead BrownPants."

Just then SpongeBob felt something in his pockets. "Hey, what's this?" he said, pulling out a bottle of bubbles and a blowing wand.

"Not bubbles!" shouted his new friends. Then they ran away!

SpongeBob started walking. Soon he found himself in New Kelp City.

Grrr! His stomach began to growl loudly. He needed food, but he didn't have a penny in his pockets! There was only one thing to do – get a job.

But his fantastic bubble-blowing skills made every employer run away in fear.

I don't understand, thought SpongeBob. Is something wrong with this place, or is it me?

45

SpongeBob began walking around the city aimlessly. To cheer himself up, he took out his trusty bubbles and began to blow. "Bubbles will steady the old nerves," he said to himself. *Bloop!* "Feeling better already!"

Then, out of the dark shadows, came a group of scary-looking fish. They were big, they were mean, and they didn't want any bubbles on their turf! They called themselves the Bubble Poppin' Boys. They tried to catch SpongeBob, so he ran away as fast as he could.

Then SpongeBob had an idea! He blew the biggest bubble ever – and caught the Bubble Poppin' Boys inside! It floated far, far away with them inside, never to return.

Citizens of New Kelp City flooded the streets with bubbles in celebration! "Thank you, Cheesehead BrownPants!" the mayor said to SpongeBob. "You have restored bubble blowing to the streets! I appoint you the new mayor!"

New Kelp Times

Cheesehead Named Mayor of New Kelp!

Meanwhile . . . Sandy, Squidward, and Patrick continued their search. "There he is!" exclaimed Sandy. "On the cover of that newspaper! He's mayor of New Kelp City? We've got to get there, quick!"

When Sandy, Patrick, and Squidward got there, they were shocked by what they saw – and heard.

"Citizens of New Kelp City," announced SpongeBob over a microphone. "I'm not exactly sure what a 'mayor' is. But, as long as I am wearing this hat, it will always be safe to blow bubbles in New Kelp City, or my name isn't . . . CheeseHead BrownPants."

"CheeseHead BrownPants?" said Sandy.

"Who are you?" asked SpongeBob.

"We're your best friends!" said Patrick.

"Sorry. All I remember is hitting my head, blowing some bubbles, and now, poof! I'm mayor!"

"You must have lost your memory when you hit your head," said Sandy. "Come back to Bikini Bottom with us. We're all real sorry we yelled at you, buddy."

"I'm sorry," replied SpongeBob. "I can't leave. I'm late for a very important meeting." With that SpongeBob hopped in the mayor's limousine, which was waiting for him.

Good thing Squidward was in the driver's seat! "Don't just stand there," he called to Sandy and Patrick. "Get in!"

And off they rode, back to Bikini Bottom.

"Start fryin' up them Patties!" yelled Mr Krabs cheerfully when he saw SpongeBob come through the door.

"I was a fry cook before?" asked SpongeBob, unimpressed.

"Yes, lad! The best in the business!" replied Mr Krabs proudly.

"Well, I'm going back to my modest job as mayor," SpongeBob announced, dropping the spatula on the floor. "New Kelp City needs me."

"Mr Krabs," cried Squidward with delight. "I brought back the number-one fry cook. You've got to pay up!"

"All right. A deal is a deal," said Mr Krabs grumpily, handing the golden egg over to Squidward.

As Squidward walked towards the door staring at his prized possession, he tripped on the spatula SpongeBob had dropped. His precious egg went soaring through the air and hit SpongeBob – *smack* – on the top of his head!

"You okay, SpongeBob?" asked Sandy.

"Just a bit of a headache, Sandy," answered SpongeBob. "Well, time to get to work!"

Patrick, Sandy, and Mr Krabs all jumped with excitement. They were thrilled to have him back!

Everyone was so happy that SpongeBob was back home!
"Order up!" he called cheerily from behind the window of the Krusty Krab kitchen.
Things were finally back to normal in Bikini Bottom!

56

by David Lewman • illustrated by Heather Martinez

"HII-EEE-YAH!" SpongeBob yelled as he lunged towards Sandy with a mighty karate strike.

Sandy easily blocked his attack. "Nice try, SpongeBob," she said, chuckling. "I think that's enough karate for today."

SpongeBob nodded. "Same time tomorrow?" he asked eagerly.

Sandy shook her head. "No can do, SpongeBob. I'm going to be grabbing my stick and carving some barrels!"

"Huh?" SpongeBob asked. He had no idea what she just said.

"I'm going surfing!" Sandy explained. "Wanna come?"

SpongeBob hesitated. "Well, I don't know . . ."

"You do know how to surf, don't you?" Sandy asked, taking off her gloves.

"Well . . . sure!" SpongeBob answered, his voice cracking a little.

"Great!" Sandy said. "I'll see you at Goo Lagoon tomorrow then. I hear there are gonna be some epic, heavy, gnarly waves!"

"Uh . . . oh, my favourite kinds," said SpongeBob, not sure what she meant.

As soon as Sandy was gone, SpongeBob cried, "Oh, Gary! What am I going to do? I told Sandy I know how to surf! But I don't know how to surf! This is a disaster!"

Patrick heard SpongeBob's cries and ran over. "Don't worry, SpongeBob!" he said cheerfully. "You may be a hodad, but I'm stoked to help you rip some tubes!"

"Huh?" SpongeBob asked. Patrick was as confusing as Sandy!

"You may be a beginner, but I'm excited to teach you to surf," Patrick explained. "That was surfer talk."

SpongeBob looked surprised. "You know how to surf, Patrick?"

Patrick smiled. "Of course I do! Why do you think I wear these cool surfer shorts all the time?"

"Because they're the only pair you own?"

"Exactly! Let's go!"

At Goo Lagoon, Patrick began SpongeBob's first lesson. "The first thing you do is—"

"STAND BACK!" shouted Larry the Lobster. The big lifeguard set a groaning surfer down on the sand.

"Wh-what happened?" SpongeBob asked anxiously.

"Dude tried to catch a bomb but ended up getting drilled in the zone," Larry replied seriously.

"Huh?" SpongeBob asked.

"He tried to surf a wave that was too big for him," Patrick explained.

Trembling, SpongeBob suggested, "Maybe we should leave."

"Why?" asked Patrick, puzzled. "Are you scared?"

SpongeBob put on a brave face. "No . . . I just don't want to run into Sandy."

Patrick shrugged. "Okay, I can teach you right in your own yard."

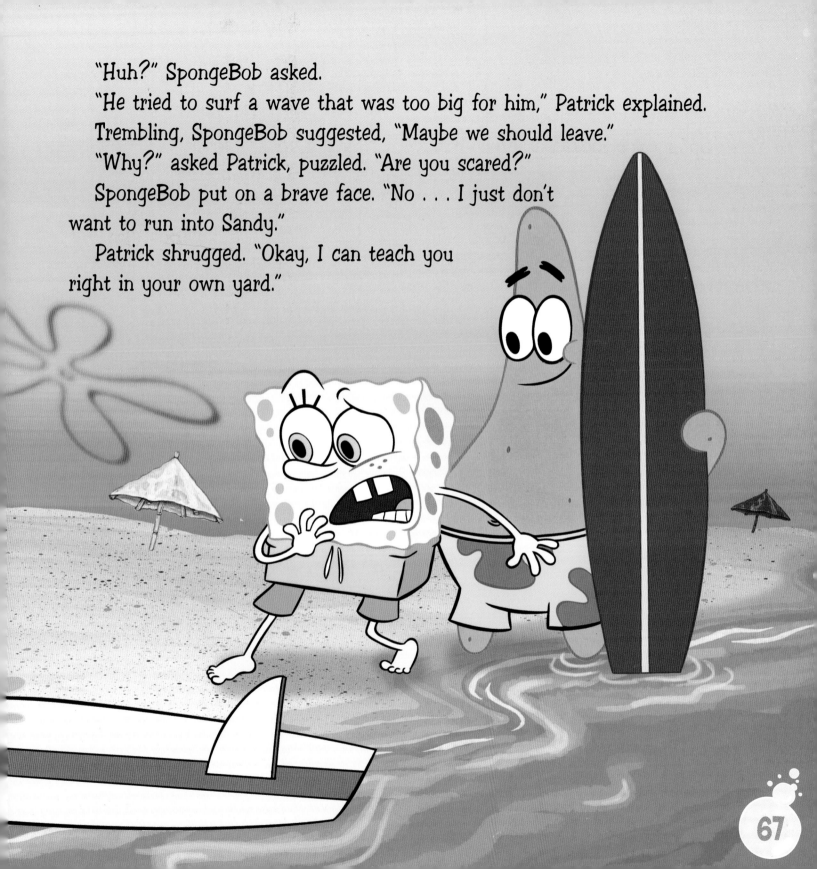

Back in SpongeBob's yard, Patrick laid his surfboard on the sand. "Okay, lie down on your stick," he said.

SpongeBob looked around. "But I don't have a stick, Patrick."

"That's what we surfers call our boards," Patrick said.

"Oh, right!" SpongeBob said. He lay down on the surfboard like it was a bed.

"Good!" said Patrick. "Except you're supposed to be on your stomach."

SpongeBob turned over. Next Patrick showed him how to paddle out to a wave, pop up, and stand on the board.

After a while SpongeBob started to get the hang of standing up on the surfboard. "I think I'm getting it, Patrick!" he said, excited. "You're a great teacher!"

Patrick smiled. "Now you just have to try it on a wave."

"Where do we get a wave?" SpongeBob asked.

Patrick thought for a moment. Then he snapped his fingers. "I know! Squidward's bathtub! Come on!"

In Squidward's bathroom Patrick called out directions. "All right! Now try a cutback towards the lip! Catch some air!"

When Squidward came home he was a little upset.

SpongeBob and Patrick spent the rest of the day cleaning up Squidward's flooded house. "I just hope I'm ready to surf with Sandy tomorrow," SpongeBob said.

"Oh, you're ready," Patrick said encouragingly. "Unless the waves are epic. Or gnarly. Or heavy. Or macking. Or—"

"Patrick," SpongeBob interrupted. "Do all those surf words mean huge?"

"Pretty much, yeah," Patrick admitted.

The next morning SpongeBob got to Goo Lagoon early. The waves were GIGANTIC. "Maybe Sandy won't show up," he said hopefully.

Just then Sandy walked up. "Ready to ride, SpongeBob? These waves are bigger than a Texas skyscraper!"

SpongeBob tried to look excited. "You know it, Sandy! I'm stoked!" he said brightly, then added to himself, "I think."

"SURF'S UP!" Sandy shouted as she charged into the water with her surfboard. "Come on, SpongeBob! I can't wait to hang ten!"

"Yes, Sandy, I also want to curl my toes over the front of my board," SpongeBob answered, proud to know what she was talking about. He took a deep breath and was about to follow Sandy when a surfer dragged himself out of the water.

"How is it out there?" SpongeBob asked.

"Awesome," the surfer answered. "And terrifying."

SpongeBob gulped. "Are you going back in?"

The surfer shook his head. "Not happenin', dude. Broke my board."

As the surfer walked sadly away with his broken surfboard, SpongeBob got an idea.

SpongeBob jumped up and down on his surfboard. If I break my board, then I *can't* go surfing! he thought. I'll be saved!

But the surfboard didn't break. "Hmm . . . this stick is tougher than I thought," SpongeBob said, stomping hard.

As he jumped, SpongeBob looked out for cracks on his board. He didn't notice that his board had slipped into the surf, and that he was being carried out towards an enormous wave!

"If I can just jump hard enough, I can break this stupid surfboard!" SpongeBob said. He had no idea that he was riding the biggest wave to ever hit Goo Lagoon!

SpongeBob kicked the surfboard. He tried standing on his hands and pulling at the tip of the board. He punched, smacked, and whacked the board — but nothing worked. This was one tough surfboard!

Finally SpongeBob gave up. "I'll just have to tell Sandy the waves are too big for me," he said, before looking up to see . . .

. . . a huge crowd on the beach — cheering for him! Sandy ran up to SpongeBob. "SpongeBob, that was fantastic! Nobody's ever ridden a wave like that before!"

"Ridden a wave?" SpongeBob asked, confused.

"You rode that humongous wave like a cowboy on a buckin' bronco!" Sandy said, grinning from ear to ear.

"I did?" SpongeBob asked. "I mean . . . yeah, I did!"

"Hooray for SpongeBob!" everyone shouted.
"Hooray for gnarly waves!" SpongeBob shouted back.

adapted by Erica Pass
based on the teleplay by Dani Michaeli and Steven Banks
illustrated by The Artifact Group

It was a perfect day for blowing bubbles. SpongeBob blew a bubble large and floaty enough to carry him and Patrick high above Bikini Bottom.

"This bubble will break all records," said SpongeBob. But he didn't realize how far they had gone until much later.

The two began to pound on the bubble. "We're never going to get out of here!" they cried.

The bubble finally coasted down and into a cave, coming to rest against something sharp. It burst, and Patrick and SpongeBob fell to the ground.

"What happened?" asked Patrick.

"*That's* what happened!" said SpongeBob, pointing at a jagged piece of metal. He got closer and saw that it said "Antis."

"What do you think that means, Pat?"

"Hmm," said Patrick. "Antis . . . antis . . . SquarePantis! It probably belonged to your ancestors! You must wear the ancient crest of your ancestors, for it is your birthright!"

And Patrick stuck the amulet in SpongeBob's head!

89

SpongeBob and Patrick decided to take it to the Bikini Bottom Museum, where they bumped into Squidward.

"Would you two watch where you're—," Squidward started to yell. Then he saw what SpongeBob had in his hand. "What are you doing with the amulet of Atlantis?" he asked. He thought they were trying to steal it from the museum!

But then Squidward realized that SpongeBob and Patrick had in fact found the missing half of the Atlantian amulet!

"What's an Atlantian omelet?" asked SpongeBob.

"Amulet!" yelled Squidward. "Not omelet! It's the key to untold riches!"

At that moment Mr Krabs showed up. "Did someone say 'untold riches'?"

Squidward told them about the lost city of Atlantis. "For reasons unknown, the great city disappeared one day, and no ruins were ever found. All the inventions you take for granted were given to us by the Atlantians."

As Squidward spoke, SpongeBob found himself staring at a bubble shown on a mural. He pointed it out to Patrick.

"That's the oldest living bubble," said Squidward. "It lives in Atlantis."

"It's the most beautiful bubble I've ever seen," said Patrick.

Just then Sandy showed up. "What's all the hubbub, boys?" she asked.

"These two chowderbrains found the missing half of the amulet of Atlantis," said Squidward.

"Well, let's hitch them two doggies up!" said Sandy.

The group watched as Squidward carefully placed the two pieces together – and they glowed!

Suddenly there was a bright beam of light and lots of rumbling — and a huge van appeared, crashing through the ceiling of the museum! The amulet began to spin. It rose up and landed in a slot on the front of the van. The doors opened up.

"Welcome aboard the sea ship *Atlantis*," a computerized voice said. "This is a nonstop trip, so please take a seat, relax, and we'll be on our way."

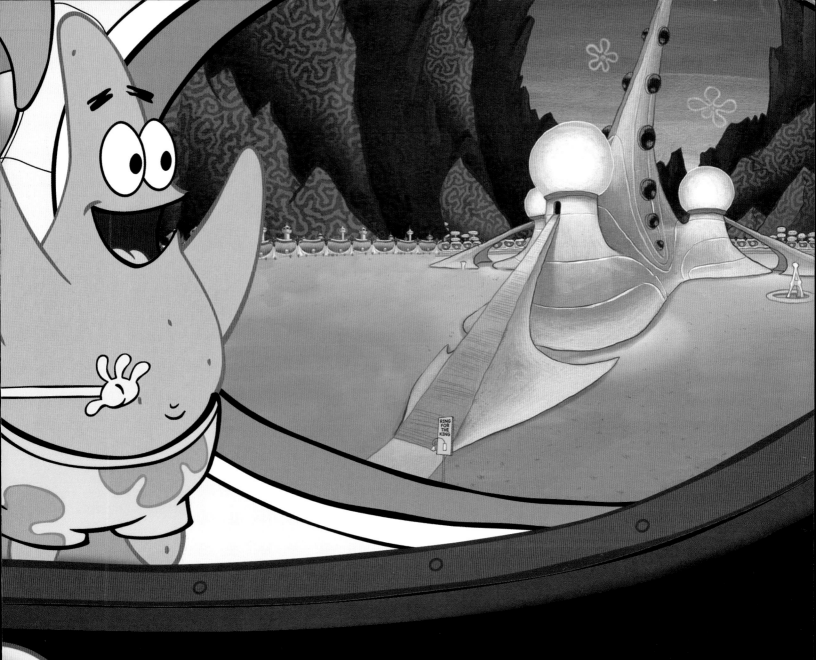

The gang coasted deep through the water until finally they could see Atlantis below. Then they hurtled toward the city and hit the ground, skidding to a stop. They emerged from the van and approached a long staircase. At the bottom was a bell.

"Go on, SpongeBob," said Mr Krabs. "Ring the bell."

SpongeBob rang the bell and everyone waited nervously as a red carpet rolled down the stairs.

"Welcome to Atlantis," a voice announced. "I've been expecting you."

With that, someone tumbled down the stairs, arriving at SpongeBob's feet. "Allow me to introduce myself," he said. "I am the Lord Royal Highness. But my friends call me LRH."

"My friends call me SpongeBob," said SpongeBob. "I'm here to see the oldest bubble."

Meanwhile Plankton had snuck aboard the bus after he overheard the group talking about the collection of weapons in Atlantis.

LRH happily showed SpongeBob and his friends around the city. "For centuries, we Atlantians spent our talents and energy building weapons to defend ourselves," he said. "But we gave up the idea of warfare long ago, and now these weapons gather dust behind these locked doors – to show what must be done if one wishes to live in harmony with all creatures of this or any world."

Next they came upon a room filled with treasure.

"Long ago we decided to focus on gathering knowledge instead of wealth," said LRH. The group followed him away from the riches, except for Mr Krabs.

Sandy was looking forward to seeing some Atlantian inventions.
"Of course," LRH said. "I give you the Atlantian Hall of Science!"
"Hoppin' acorns!" said Sandy when she saw the room filled with
machines. One machine even took objects and turned them into ice cream!
Sandy decided to stay behind in the Hall of Science.

At the Hall of Arts, Squidward couldn't believe his eyes. "The creativity! The artistry!" he cried out. "Looks like I'll be here inspiring these Atlantian art makers with my beauty. You guys go on ahead!"

"Excuse me, sir," SpongeBob said to LRH. "Can we see the bubble now?"

"Of course you can!" said LRH. "But first, please remember the bubble is more than one million years old."

SpongeBob and Patrick ran towards the bubble, which was held within a large glass ball.

"So ancient, so floaty," said SpongeBob admiringly. "It's the most beautiful, wrinkled-up, dusty old bubble I've ever seen."

"Like a delicate air raisin!" said Patrick.

LRH had to get ready for dinner. "I'm going to leave you two friendly strangers alone with our most beloved, ancient, and fragile Atlantian relic," he said as he walked away.

In their excitement, SpongeBob and Patrick pushed against the glass ball and set it loose. They struggled under its weight, finally setting it straight. And the bubble had not burst!

"That was a close one, buddy," said SpongeBob. "We should go before something else happens."

"Let's get a picture for our scrapbooks before we leave," said Patrick.

"Great idea, Pat!" SpongeBob agreed.

But it turned out to be anything *but* a great idea when the flash from the camera made the bubble burst!

SpongeBob and Patrick were panicking when they arrived for dinner. "We have to go back to Bikini Bottom now," they said.

"Why would you want to leave a paradise like this?" Squidward asked.

"Because," said SpongeBob, stalling, "I miss Gary . . . and–"

"We destroyed your most prized possession!" Patrick blurted out.

SpongeBob and Patrick were ready for LRH to start yelling at them.

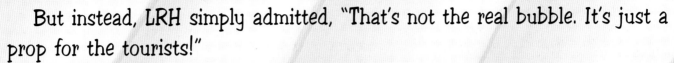

But instead, LRH simply admitted, "That's not the real bubble. It's just a prop for the tourists!"

He took out a small jar with a wrinkled bubble floating inside. "This is the real deal," he said proudly.

"Ooohh," said SpongeBob and Patrick, relieved and thrilled at the same time. Then Patrick took another picture – and the bubble burst!

This time LRH was furious. "Summon the royal guard!" he roared. "Seize the hostile bubble poppers!"

"Let's hightail it out of here!" called Sandy.

With the guards chasing them, the Bikini Bottom gang ran – until they crashed into a large tank.

Suddenly a voice from inside the machine announced, "I am in control of the most powerful weapon in Atlantis! Now bow before the new king of Atlantis, and prepare to taste my wrath!"

It was Plankton! He hopped on a button and . . . SPLURT! Ice cream oozed onto everyone below.

"Mmm . . . thanks, Plankton!" Patrick said between mouthfuls of ice cream. Plankton jumped out of the machine and kicked it, muttering to himself.

LRH was delighted. "Look, a talking speck!" he said. "It will make a fantastic replacement for our recently deflated national treasure."

As Plankton ranted and raved in a jar, LRH said goodbye to the visitors from Bikini Bottom. He seemed very eager to see them leave.

"So nice to meet you all," said LRH. "I hope you have a safe journey home. Do come back anytime."

adapted by Kim Ostrow
illustrated by Clint Bond and Andy Clark
Based on the teleplay The Great Snail Race by
Paul Tibbitt, Kent Osborne, and Merriwether Williams

It was a sunny morning in Bikini Bottom. A mailman knocked on Squidward's front door. "Aha!" said Squidward. "I can't believe it's finally here."

The mailman glanced at Squidward's signature. "Thank you, Mister . . . mmmmm . . . Tennis Balls."

"That's Tentacles!" corrected Squidward.

"Hey, check out Squidward's new snail," said Patrick.

"Looks like Gary has a new playmate," said SpongeBob.

Squidward rolled his eyes. "I wouldn't let Snellie here play with your mongrel mutt. See? Snellie even has her own pedigree papers. So if you'll excuse us, she has to start her training for Bikini Bottom's Snail Race. She'll be winning this Sunday."

"Well, I guess I can't enter Gary in that," said SpongeBob. "Sunday's laundry day!"

Squidward sighed. "You can't enter Gary because Gary isn't a purebred! But Snellie has papers!" he said. He shoved his fancy document towards SpongeBob.

"Hmmm . . . 'Property of Squidward Tentpoles,'" Patrick read.

"That's Tentacles!" corrected Squidward.

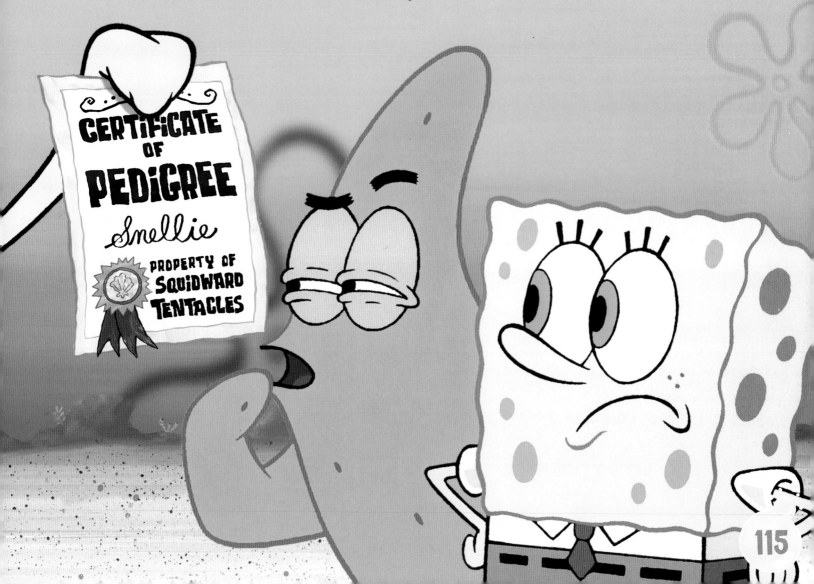

CERTIFICATE OF PEDIGREE

Snellie

PROPERTY OF SQUIDWARD TENTACLES

"Patrick, are you thinking what I'm thinking?" asked SpongeBob.

"Yeah," said Patrick. "I should get a snail and enter it in that race and beat Squidward."

"No, no, no!" shouted SpongeBob. "I'm thinking of entering Gary in that race and beating Squidward's snail."

SpongeBob had a lot of work to do to whip Gary into shape. First, he made a nutritional smoothie for his snail.

"Meow," said Gary.

"Well, of course I expect you to eat this," said SpongeBob. "It's scientifically designed to help you win tomorrow."

Gary took one look at the drink and slithered out of the room.

Patrick came over to show SpongeBob his new snail.

"Your snail is a rock," said SpongeBob.

"Yeah, I know," said Patrick proudly. "He's got nerves of steel. See you at the race!"

SpongeBob realized the competition was getting fierce.

SpongeBob blew his whistle. "Let's start with some sprints. On your mark, get set, go!"

Gary barely moved.

"Come on, Gary!" shouted SpongeBob. "You've gotta start training if you're going to win." Just then Squidward peeked in.

"Don't waste your breath, SpongeBob. That mongrel of yours doesn't have a chance," Squidward said confidently.

"All right, Gary, no more fooling around," instructed SpongeBob. "Come on, move it! Up, up, up! Down, down, down! Faster, faster, faster! Go, go, go!"

The day of the race finally arrived.

"Well, SpongeBob, I didn't think your mongrel mutt would even find the starting line," sniggered Squidward. "Congratulations."

"Save it for the loser's circle," said SpongeBob. "Gary happens to be in the best shape of his life."

Gary coughed and wheezed.

SpongeBob gave Gary his final pep talk. "Listen up. You're the undersnail. Everybody's already counting you out. Now, get out there and win!"

"Meow," muttered Gary.

"On your mark!" shouted the referee. "Get set! Slither!"

"And they're off," said the announcer. "Number six, Snellie, rockets out of the starting box, leaving the other two competitors in the dust."

"Go, Snellie! You got it, baby!" cheered Squidward.

SpongeBob was not having the same luck. Gary hadn't budged from the starting gate.

"What are you doing, Gary?" shouted SpongeBob. "The race has started. Let's go! Start moving! You're blowing everything we trained for!"

Patrick's snail was also at the starting line. "It's okay, Rocky," Patrick said. "You go when you feel like it."

Gary slowly began to move. He panted heavily as he trudged ahead. "Not good enough!" shouted his coach. "Faster!"

The more SpongeBob yelled, the faster Gary tried to go. But it was no use. Gary was exhausted.

"That coach is pushing that snail too hard," said the announcer.

Suddenly, Gary's bloodshot eye popped like a tyre!
"It looks like number seven has a blowout," said the announcer.
Shortly after, Gary's other eye blew.

"Make that two, folks," said the announcer.

"Uh . . . Gary, you can stop now," said SpongeBob.

Gary began to spin out of control — and headed straight for the wall! BAM! The crowd gasped.

"Nooooooo!" shouted SpongeBob. "Hold on, Gary, I'm coming!"

SpongeBob raced to Gary's side.

"One of the coaches has raced onto the track. That is an automatic disqualification. Looks like number six has this race all wrapped up, ladies and gentlemen," said the announcer.

Squidward cheered. "Come on, Snellie. It's all you!"

"Oh, Gary," cried SpongeBob. "Why didn't you just say I was pushing you too hard?"

"Meow," said Gary.

"You did?" asked SpongeBob. "Oh, Gary, why didn't you tell me I wasn't listening?"

"Meow," answered Gary.

"You did? Oh, Gary!" wailed SpongeBob.

Suddenly, Squidward's prize snail stopped racing. She turned to look at Gary and then rushed to his side. The two snails looked into each other's eyes and purred.

"My oh my, folks," said the announcer. "I've never seen anything quite like it. It seems Snellie, the leader, just went back to comfort Gary."

"Looks like you and me are in-laws. Eh, Squidward?" said SpongeBob.

The crowd cheered as the winner crossed the finish line.

"But that's impossible," said Squidward. "If Snellie didn't win, then who did?"

"And the winner is," shouted the announcer, "Rocky!"

The crowd went wild! Patrick started to laugh until he cried.

Squidward moaned. "My purebred, which cost me seventeen hundred dollars, lost to a rock."

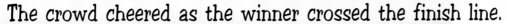

133

Patrick rushed to Squidward's side. "Don't worry, Squidward. I know how much you wanted to win, so I had the trophy engraved to you."

Squidward took the trophy in his tentacles. "Gosh, Patrick, thanks!" He looked at the plaque and read it out loud. "'The first-place snail racing cup presented to Squidward Tortellini.'"

Patrick and SpongeBob happily put their arms around their friend. "Will I ever win?" grumbled Squidward.

SQUIDWARD
TORTELLINI

by Erica Pass
illustrated by The Artifact Group

"Hey, Gary, guess what?" said SpongeBob one morning. "Today's the annual Dad and Kid Games Day at Mussel Beach."

"Meow?" asked Gary.

"That's right, Gary," said SpongeBob. "It's a whole day for dads and their kids to play games and have fun together. And my dad's coming!"

When SpongeBob got to the beach almost all of Bikini Bottom was already there.

"I'm ready!" said SpongeBob. "Squidward, are you excited?"

"Oh, thrilled to bits," said Squidward.

"Patrick, are you excited?" asked SpongeBob.

"Yes," said Patrick. "I love the beach!"
"Mr Krabs, are you excited?" SpongeBob asked.
"I'm excited to win the grand prize," said Mr Krabs.

"Prize?" said SpongeBob. "You mean there's a prize besides the joy of spending the day with our dads?"

"Of course, SpongeBob," said Sandy. "This is a contest. Only one team can win the prize. But the prize is a surprise. No one knows what it is."

"Well, I hope it's a vacation to take me far, far away from here," Squidward said.

"I don't care about the prize," said SpongeBob. "I'm just excited to be with my dad."

Just then they heard *honk-honk!* A bus filled with everyone's dads arrived at the beach.

"Hooray for dads!" SpongeBob called out.

Welcome Dads + Kids!

"Dad!" yelled SpongeBob. "It's so good to see you!"

"You, too, son," said SpongeBob's dad.

"Howdy, Sandy!" said Sandy's dad.

"Pappy! You look finer than a jackrabbit at a fancy dress ball," said Sandy.

"Oh, Pearl, isn't this exciting?" asked Mr Krabs.

"Uh, yeah, sure, Dad," replied Pearl, looking bored. "I'm *so* excited."

"Hello, Squidward," said Squidward's dad. "At least it's not raining."

"Yeah," said Squidward.

"Patrick," said Patrick's dad. "The beach!"

"I know!" yelled Patrick. "I love the beach!"

"Gather around, everyone," said Kip Kelp, host of the event. "Welcome to our annual Dad and Kid Games Day. It's wonderful to see so many of our fine citizens out here for what's sure to be a great day, filled with teamwork and sportsmanship."

"Yeah, yeah, yeah," said Squidward. "Get to the good stuff."

"There will be many contests all day long," continued Kip, "and at the end we have a very special prize for the team that has won the most events."

"Did you hear that, Pearl?" Mr Krabs asked his daughter. "That prize is ours."

"Just please don't embarrass me!" said Pearl.

The first competition was a relay race, which Sandy and her dad won.

"I knew I could count on you, Pappy!" said Sandy. "We're on our way to winning that prize!"

"Sandy," said SpongeBob, "there are more important things than winning."

"I think not," said Squidward.

Next was a competition to see which team could blow the most bubbles.
"Ha!" said Mr Krabs. "My Pearl is an expert bubble-blower!"
Pearl sighed. "If I have to do this, I may as well win," she said.
SpongeBob and his dad blew beautiful bubbles, not caring about how many there were. Patrick and his dad went to look for buried treasure.

Squidward and his dad ended up blowing the most bubbles. "Prize, here I come!" he called out.

"Not so fast, Squid," said Sandy. "You haven't won the grand prize yet."

In the next contest teams had to build sand castles. Squidward hurried to build a really tall tower – but it came crashing down just before time was up.

"See?" Sandy said to Squidward. "You'd better calm down, or else that prize is mine!"

SpongeBob was all set for the jellyfish roundup. "Come on, Dad!" he said. "Jellyfish love me! And I love them!"

In no time SpongeBob and his dad had gathered the most jellyfish.

"Nice work, SpongeBob," said Sandy. "You just might win the grand prize!"

"Really?" asked SpongeBob.

"Still don't care about that prize, SpongeBob?" asked Squidward. "I heard it's something you've been wanting for a while . . ."

"You heard it's a gold-plated spatula?" asked SpongeBob.

"Maybe," said Squidward.

"Oh, Dad," said SpongeBob. "I've been wanting a gold-plated spatula forever! We *have* to win now."

"But SpongeBob," said his dad. "I thought this day was all about spending time with the people you love."

"Right," said SpongeBob. "And I love spatulas. Let's go!"

The next competition was a badminton tournament, and SpongeBob did his best to try to win. He frantically ran circles around his dad, huffing and puffing and tripping in the sand.

"Out of my way!" SpongeBob yelled.

"You know, Son," said SpongeBob's dad, "there are more important things than winning."

"Of course there are," SpongeBob replied. "Like what I can do with that golden spatula! I can already feel it working its fry magic in my hand."

SpongeBob's dad sighed. "Oh, SpongeBob."

There were many more contests, and by the end of the day everyone was tired out – except Patrick and his dad, who had just woken up from a nap. They were in time to hear Kip Kelp announce the winner of the grand prize.

"This has been an inspiring Dad and Kid Games Day," said Kip. "I want to thank you all for coming out to compete. It truly shows the spirit—"

"Come on, already!" yelled Squidward. "Who won?"

"Okay," Kip said. "The winning team is . . . Plankton and his dad!"

Plankton hopped up onto the stage, excited. "What did we win?" he asked. "Is it the secret recipe?"

"No," said Kip, "you've won the honour of having your names inscribed on a plaque that will be placed in a new rock and coral garden in the centre of town."

"Uh . . . that's it?" asked Plankton. "I ran around in circles all day long for this?"

Hearing Plankton's words, SpongeBob turned to his dad. "Oh, Dad, I'm sorry," he said. "I lost sight of what it means to be able to spend time with you."

"That's all right, SpongeBob," said his dad. "We all want to win sometimes. But you know what, I had a great time just being with you."

"Yeah, me too, Dad," said SpongeBob.

"Everyone is welcome to come to the Krusty Krab," Mr Krabs announced.

"For free Krabby Patties?" asked Patrick.

"Never!" said Mr Krabs. "But everyone can help themselves to as many napkins as they like."

"Woo-hoo!" said SpongeBob. "Dad, who needs a gold-plated spatula when I have you?"